If you would like to get in touch with Steve to ask a question or to enquire about having Steve speak at your church or event, please visit www.steveavery.co.uk

FROM DARKNESS TO LIGHT

ISBN 978-1-914458-21-7

First Published April 2023
By P2D Books Ltd

Printed and bound in Great Britain by
www.p2dbooks.co.uk
Westoning

— *Introduction* —

Many people have only heard of Jesus, knowing little about his life. Others, who have known some of the stories concerning the greatest man in history, have never encountered the reality of why he came and lived on earth for a short time of only 33 years.

Steve could well have been in one of those groups, living his life in the best way he knew, motivated by the lusts and treats life throws up, giving little regard to where he was heading. His choices were leading down a pathway to hell and, though he didn't realise it, his quest for the trappings of financial success were speeding that journey on.

Steve's life one day would take a dramatic turn – one that could have ruined many a man.

It was a journey one would not wish on anybody; nevertheless events combined mysteriously to bring about a radical change.

This is a gripping story, one in which Steve met with the one Jesus said he would send – the Holy Spirit. Or was this combination of events just coincidental? That is for the reader to decide.

Steve's life could not have sunk any lower, but the transformation he encountered supernaturally is an inspiration that should invigorate any reader towards the faith that comes through an encounter with the Lord.

Steve's life story isn't just about himself, it contains something precious for you; a personal message so profound it should grip you like a vice. Yet it's a message with a marvellous outcome that shows the nature of a loving God who wants to reach into a willing heart.

Meet the family

My name is Steve Avery, and this is my life story; a story about the choices I have made. Some of those choices were good but a lot were unwise at best; terrible or stupid at worst.

I was born in January 1953 at South Moulton, in North Devon. I have one brother, Vince, who is six years older than me. My father, Derek, or Sid, depending on which time of his life you met him, had a sister and twin brothers; his family lived in South Moulton. My mother, Mary, and her family came from Fleetwood, in Lancashire.

My mum's dad was a trawler skipper. His boat worked out of Fleetwood into the North Sea. All I remember about Grandad is he was a big bloke known as Mad Jack. When he retired he was a taxi driver. He smoked Capstan Full Strength Cigarettes and in his bedroom he had a buoy that he used as an ashtray. He died of cancer.

Devon was a farming community, rationing was just coming to an end so if you had plenty, you ate well after so long of very little. Grandma was a big lady and Mum lived with them when she was expecting me, so I started out as a fat kid and that set things later in my life as you will see as we go through this story. We moved around a lot as Dad was an engineer in the Fleet Air Arm stationed in different areas. He served on aircraft carriers and spent quite a lot of time away from home in the early part of my life.

My parents had met when he was on leave. My father had gone back to sea when my mother discovered she was pregnant with my brother. As you can imagine in 1947 it was frowned upon. Dad was working his way up through the ranks and was told to go and "do the right thing" or it would affect his career. So he did and they got married. I don't think he ever really forgave her or my brother though.

My first real memories of home were in Gosport near Portsmouth, Hampshire; we stayed there until I was six or seven. We lived next to Fort Brockenhurst and as kids we used to play in the fort. How things have changed! We would go out in the morning with a packed lunch and play for hours. I was only four but my brother was meant to look after me. I think this might be quite common, especially with the first child.

The first day at primary school was horrible. I couldn't wait to get this interruption to my life over with and can remember coming home slapping my hands together, saying "glad that's over" and not wanting to ever go back again.

At around that time my brother was sent off to a naval boarding school for boys, on the east coast near Ipswich, which was okay with me as it gave me a better life with my mum. We would go and visit him once a term on a Sunday and take him out for a couple of hours. He was told, and so was I, what a great privilege it was to go to such a great school with few pupils per class and a high standard of education. The majority of the fees being paid by the Navy, the education was second to none. The only downside from my point of view was being told I would go there when I was old enough. So at the age of five, just starting out on an educational journey that I didn't really want to be involved in, I had the prospect, on reaching eleven, of being sent away for months at a time to a place I didn't want to go to, with hundreds of boys I didn't want to be with - and no prospect of avoiding this fate.

When I was about seven years old my dad was transferred to the Royal Aircraft Establishment at Farnborough, in Hampshire. We moved from Gosport to an RAF station at Odiham and lived in the officer's quarters. We even had a man that would come and help clean. I hated moving because I had to meet new people and start again at a new school and felt like an outsider. Also being a fat kid didn't help. I can remember having to walk quite a long way between the fields from the camp to the village school. We didn't stay there very long because once my father had settled into work at the RAE my parents bought a bungalow in a place called Ash near Aldershot, about four miles from his work.

Dad liked the bungalow and the garden to look immaculate. I remember he painted all the inside walls of the bungalow white and said we could have whatever colour we liked as long as it was white! All the paths around the bungalow had edging stones which were also painted white. The grass was a perfect length, it didn't have weeds, it was rolled flat and had lines up and down because the mower had a big roller on the back. The grass had to be cut in the same direction each time to keep the lines intact. The real downside of this was we were not allowed to walk on the grass or play in the garden, if you did he would know, because we would leave foot marks.

We lived opposite a pub and next to that was a recreation field which had swings. Behind that were miles and miles of army ranges and land they used for military exercises. When there were red flags flying we were not meant to go on the land, which made it more of an adventure! My friends and I would spend time on the ranges looking for ammunition for our pretend fights. We found some 303 cases which we used as ammunition in our catapults. One day we were hiding in trenches shooting at each other with these cartridge cases as ammo when my friend stuck his head up just as I fired and the case stuck in his forehead just above his eyes. I got in loads of trouble over that one.

I used to call my dad “sir”. This was the sort of relationship we had. Being an officer for a long time. He loved Jaguar cars and drinking in the Officers’ Mess. He had a large double garage and workshop built in the garden. On the weekends he would service people’s cars, mainly naval officers; he was always bringing them home. He loved to take people for a drink in the pub opposite and and then bring them home. My mother never knew who might turn up with him and he expected her to feed and entertain his guests. By now my brother was away most of the time at boarding school and I was going to the local junior school. I was about nine years old and had put on more weight. My nickname was Barrel. To try and make up for this I decided to become a bit of a joker rather than studying: I just messed about for the next couple of years because I knew I was going to boarding school when I was eleven and couldn’t think of a way of getting out of it.

When my brother came home from boarding school at the age of 16 Dad gave him the choice of becoming a mechanic or a ladies hairdresser. He chose to become a ladies hairdresser. He wasn’t back long before it was time for me to go - the next major interruption to my life.

The Royal Hospital School, Holbrook

Boarding school

When I was 11 my mother accompanied me on the train from Ash Vale Station to Waterloo and then across London to Kings Cross station to put me on the School Special with hundreds of other boys. I can remember crying my heart out, begging her not to do this to me, I then remember being handed over to someone on the train and trying to plan a way out of this, hoping it was a bad dream and I'd wake up and be at home.

When I got to the school with all the other boys we were shown to the houses we had been allocated. All the houses were large and named after famous Warships: I was in Hood House. I can't remember how many boys were in each house; there was a junior side and a senior side. We had to sleep in a dormitory with many other boys and my space was a bed and a locker. The next day we took an entrance exam, so I thought in my naivety that if I purposely failed this, they would send me home. That didn't work. We were issued with our naval uniforms which were made from a serge material and included short trousers. My legs used to split with the cold wind as we were right on the east coast and the material of the uniform was so rough.

The day started with a coldish shower, we would then march to breakfast. We ate in a large dining room. There were red lights around the room which came on when the food was being served or cleared. If the lights were on no talking was allowed. The senior boys sat at the top of the table and served the food, the junior boys sat at the bottom of the table. This meant that the nice food such as chips would be taken before it reached the junior boys. This was very important to a fat kid like me.

In some ways it was an excellent school. The class size was very low and the standard of education was very high. All this is great if you're sensible and can take advantage of the benefits, however, as the saying goes, you can take a horse to water but you can't make it drink. The days were quite busy and there were plenty of sports that you could join in with if you wanted; things like rugby, football, shooting, swimming, sailing, and cross country, none of which I really enjoyed. I played a bit of rugby; quite liked shooting and swimming, but hated cross country. Each term I had a diary and would number the days down backwards until I could go home and cross them off as another day served. We used to have to spit and polish our shoes, press our uniforms and generally keep ourselves busy. We would play table tennis in our spare time.

I got interested in telling ghost stories. We started getting interested in spooky things, like trying to levitate one of our mates. Some of us would sit around him, put a finger each under him and try and lift him up off the ground. I don't think it ever worked properly, but I felt it should have worked.

I hated being at school and was determined to get out of this prison somehow. At that time the cane and the slipper were still widely used. I seemed to get either the slipper or the stick on a regular basis. It built up anger, bitterness, resentment, rejection and quite a tough backside .The masters could give you the cane but we were told they had to have a gap of three days between canings to allow your behind to recover. The older boys who were Petty Officers and Chief Petty officers had their own common rooms. They could give you the slipper - when they did, they made you stand with your head under the door knob so if you raised your head you would hit it on the door knob. It took me some time and quite a few bad reports before it was suggested that it would be better all-round if my parents put me somewhere else. On my last report, when I was 13 years and 6 months old, the headmaster's comments were written in red: "Unsatisfactory on all sides: I have warned him that if he is to continue to justify a place here at all there must to be a radical improvement next term, when he will also stay on report."

Finally after two years, I was out. My dad was so angry.

I started at a secondary modern school a few miles away from home. I had come from this very strict boarding school, to a mixed school which I still didn't want to be in. Secondary modern school seemed like mayhem with people all over the place. I managed to get the stick from the headmaster a couple of times and almost felt sorry for him as, compared to boarding school, it didn't hurt. The trouble was that I had been in a very tough regime and suddenly, as far as I was concerned, there was no discipline.

Need for speed

I bought my first scramble bike which was a 197cc Villiers. I was fourteen at the time so I kept it hidden over the ranges and would go on it after school and at weekends until someone found it and handed it into the police. I managed to get it back with just a warning and the policeman was good enough to collect it from the police station and bring it home for me in a van.

I had two uncles who were twins: one was into the theatre and the other one was a painter - as in artist - and I think he was in the magic circle, whenever they visited they would perform party magic tricks. They had lived in London and Paris and my father didn't have much to do with them. He was working his way up through the ranks and each time he got promotion, he got in with his bosses. At that time they still got a rum ration and a cigarette ration. So Dad drank and smoked and was always at the Officer's mess or going to parties. After he had got drunk he would drive home. He made a block of wood that fitted under the accelerator to stop him going too fast! He loved Jaguar cars which he would buy and sell.

On the weekends, my father would work in our garage on people's cars, so on Saturday mornings I had to work in the garage for four hours and got paid for this. On Sunday I had to work for nothing for the good of the house. I also got a job working after school in an electrical shop in the village. I would help rebuild washing machines and then on Saturdays servicing and cleaning cars for my dad. I used to back the cars in and out the garage and that's how I started to learn how to drive. Dad always had people's cars at home so one day after Mum and Dad had left for work I borrowed a Mini Cooper that was in the garage and drove it to school with two other boys! We went the long way round to go to school through the army ranges and I nearly hit an army lorry, as I went round a corner. Anyway I parked the car next to the school and drove it home afterwards, parked it back in the garage and got away with it.

At school, because I had not come up directly from junior school to senior school I felt like an outsider. I can remember I used to stand in our kitchen which was at the front of the bungalow and watch the boys and girls across the playing field hanging round the swings. My mum used to ask, "why don't you go across and join in?" Part of me really wanted to but I didn't feel that I could. Even writing this reminds me of the conflict that was going on inside of me. There were definitely two voices and they didn't agree with each other. How many times do we stand at a situation when we have to make a decision, a choice? Some of those choices might be minor and some major, but the direction our lives take depends on these choices.

Instead, I used to go into the back garden get my air rifle out and shoot at anything that moved.

I hung around with the boys from the estate behind our house and felt I needed to do things that other people didn't do. I borrowed a 125cc scooter and went with two friends to Frensham Ponds, near Farnham which was about 10 miles away. I wore my brother's three-quarter-length suede coat. I could hardly keep up with my friends as their bikes were bigger and faster. We turned down a road towards the ponds and they pulled away from me. I could see in the distance they had stopped and they were talking so I decided I would really scare them by going flat out between the two of them. They looked horrified and fell apart just like a Tom and Jerry show as I beeped my horn and tore up between them. It was then I realised why they had stopped: the road came to an end and that point and became a sand track. As soon as the bike hit the sand it stopped but I didn't. I had no helmet on. There was a barbed wire fence on the left-hand side and as I flew along it my brother's suede coat was ripped down the back from top to bottom. We managed to get the bike back on the road and get home without any further incidents. My brother never knew what happened to his coat.

I thought I was tough. It must have been hormones - or just stupidity. My part-time job repairing and rebuilding secondhand washing machines in the village ended. I couldn't resist helping myself to some of the takings to play the pinball machines in the cafés. The man who ran the electrical shop found out and sacked me.

I was 14 when Mum and Dad went out for the evening to the officers' mess for a dinner and dance. I took a car from the garage. It was a 4 litre Austin Vanden Plas that Dad was working on; a big car with leather seats. I couldn't see over the steering wheel easily, so when I drove it was more comfortable to look through the steering wheel than over it. I had arranged to pick up a mate from near the school. We then drove around and picked up a couple more. We needed some petrol so all pitched together to get some petrol - how stupid can you be? - we went into a petrol station in this big posh car; five schoolboys put five pounds' worth of petrol in using small change. We drove along the A30 near Camberley in Surrey. I can remember getting faster and faster, the boy sitting next to me reading the speedo: 70… 80… 90… we managed to get up to 100 mph before I bottled. Someone had reported us. We had two police cars chasing us. They stopped us; one car pulled up on the inside to stop anyone getting out and the other one boxed us in on the outside. They arrested us and took us all to Camberley police station. My father turned up to get me after the police went to the dinner and dance to get him. When he got there he was so angry. Looking back on it now I don't blame him. I had to go to the headmaster; I think my dad came with me to watch as I got the stick. The police took me to court: I got fined and endorsements on my licence. In fact I had five endorsements and a year-long ban. I was only 15 when I was banned, before I got a licence, which meant I got my licence back a month or so after my 16th birthday.

In January 1968 when I was 15 the headmaster called me in and told me to leave. I can't remember whether I left in the January or at the end of the school year. I think it was January because they couldn't wait to get rid of me. My dad gave me careers advice: "get a job". He gave me two options. The first was a ladies' hairdresser (like my brother who had taken that option and worked in Guildford for a well-known hairdresser) or an apprentice mechanic. I took the second option and he got me an apprenticeship in a garage called Tourist Trophy in Farnham in Surrey. I think it was a five year apprenticeship, my first week's wages were £3.30 in todays money which I had to take home and give to my parents, they gave me pocket money back. I was smoking by then so I needed all the money I could get my hands on.

I would walk over a mile to get a train to Farnham then had to walk to the garage which was on the other side of town. Sometimes I rode my pushbike the five miles instead. When I got off the train I would go to the café opposite and play on the pinball machines. I also used to hang around another café and got friendly with some older boys who had cars. To be part of that scene I would supply them with parts for their cars which I would get from the garage spares department, I passed my motorbike test one month after I got my licence back and bought my first motorbike, a Triumph Tiger Cub.

The first day I could legally use the bike I was taking the first part of my City and Guilds exam. I didn't have to go to work before taking the exam at Farnborough Technical College so I decided to go across and meet my friend Bob who worked with me. He lived in Aldershot. We went back over to Farnborough and a place called North Camp. Bob was on his scooter. I can remember going down Lynchford Road overtaking Bob and looking over my shoulder laughing at him when his expression changed. I had seen that expression on people's faces before. As I turned round I realised why: the car in front of me had stopped. I hit his boot and went straight over the back of the car onto the roof, bounced off that and landed on the road. My knees and my hands were cut a bit, the bike was a bit damaged and I was a bit dazed but, other than that, I was ok. Bob helped me put the bike in someone's garden. He told the man he would look after me and he put me on the back of his scooter. We turned around, went back up the road, but as we got to the T junction about 300 yards further up the road a car pulled across in front of us and we hit it. Bob managed to hang onto the bike but in my slightly dazed state I went across the road and ended up sliding under a lorry that just stopped. I can remember lying there thinking, "I don't want to get up". I remember people pulling me out from under the lorry. There was an army doctor who came to help: he cut my jeans up the leg so he could see the cuts on my knees. My elbows and hands were cut, bruised and hurting. Bob managed to get his scooter going and said he was going to work… at that moment the police turned up and asked who I was and who Bob was. I told them the truth but Bob had given them a false name and address. As I was giving them different details they didn't believe me so they wouldn't take me to the hospital; they took me to the police station instead and still didn't believe me. When they finally found out I was telling the truth they took me to the local cottage hospital to get me patched up so I could get to the college. In fact they took me home to get changed and dropped me off at the college. I passed my exam!

When I was 17 I passed my driving test straight away. I drove a Mini which I had rebuilt over the months before my birthday. I had only driven this for a month or so when I wrote the car off. I was chasing a mate in his car when I slid off the road into a security fence and flattened a railway warning sign. I was always buying, repairing and selling cars. I was not interested in doing a good job; only in making money. I didn't care how badly the cars were repaired or how they went, as long as I made money from them. This went on for years until a bloke got caught with a radio I had sold him and gave the police my name. They came and arrested me for supplying stolen goods from the garage stores. The boss decide to make an example of me: he sacked me from my apprenticeship, and the police took me to court. My solicitor said because of my previous offences I would definitely expect to do time in prison. It went to court and I was found guilty, however when the magistrate was summing up he didn't ask if I had any previous convictions and I got a suspended sentence.

A deal with the devil

When I was 19 I managed to persuade my parents to let me have use of the flat which was over the bakery they owned. My dad couldn't wait to get me out of his house because I was always in trouble: I drank, smoked and did drugs and stole money to supply my habits. I knew I needed to get a job but because I'd been sacked it was difficult. I saw that the North Sea oil rigs were hiring people and paid more money than I could ever imagine. The only problems were: I was scared of heights, and I didn't want to work too hard. They were working six weeks on and four weeks off… but the money was the big draw.

I was always short of money and over the years had managed to find a way to get money. My friends now were into drugs and heavy rock music. I had friends who were into magic and spiritual things. I was still very interested in spiritual things. When I was in boarding school we went to church regularly but I knew these people tended to talk in a way that was not normal and the words they used didn't seem to have any relevance to modern living and didn't seem to have any power. If there was no power in the church, what was the point in trying to be good? So I looked at magic and the occult instead. I started to go to psychics to get my cards read and went to palmists to try and find out what was going to happen in my future: hopefully I was going to have a good time and get lots of money.

As you can see up to this point I had made a few bad decisions but now I knew things were getting worse. The last psychic I went to was in autumn 1972. She turned over the death card and said I was going to be involved in an accident, she said someone would die but

I would get a lot of money. I used to have dreams about being killed in a car accident so I didn't have an expectation of getting old. I watched a film called Vanishing Point: It's a film about two guys who delivered cars in America. They are on speed and drive these cars from state to state. The police keep trying to stop them. The film finishes with the main character dying as he notices a roadblock too late. It seemed to confirm to me that I would die young.

As I needed money I applied to the oil companies that worked on the North Sea oil rigs and, as I thought I was psychic, I believed I would get the job. I told my friends this is what I was going to do, but really I didn't want to do it. I was really worried about going to the North Sea on the rigs. I was trying to think of ways of getting out of it without losing face. In the meantime I tried another channel to get money and took a job topping trees. It was a way to keep fit and get over my fear of heights. One night I had worked all day and went out to a nightclub in the evening. By the time I got back to my flat I'd had a few drinks, taken some speed and smoked some dope to get me back down after the speed.

I had to do something so I decided to try and do a deal with the devil. As far as I could tell Satan had all the power, because when I looked at the church nothing seemed to happen, whereas when you played around with magic and mind games there seemed to be a power. I got into my bedroom and started to invoke Satan to talk to me because I wanted to do a deal for money. Suddenly the room went cold and I heard a voice saying to me: "What do you want?"

The hairs on the back of my neck stood up and I can remember thinking I've overstepped the mark this time. I said, "I want money".

He said, "how much do you want?"

I thought for a moment and said £25,000, which was a lot of money for a nineteen year old.

He said: “That’s a lot of money,” which it was in 1972. He continued, “what are you going to offer me?”

I asked “what do you want?”

He replied: “I want your soul.”

I told him ''no, he couldn’t have my soul.''

He said: “You called me, you make an offer”.

At this point I should tell you that I hated disabilities but I was desperate not to go to the rigs so I offered: “You can have the use of my right arm: you can’t have my right arm but you can have the use of it.”

He said: “Okay, but £25,000 is a lot of money. What else are you going to offer me?”

We discussed a few things and I said: “You can have the use of my memory.” He then told me “£25,000 is a lot of money… I tell you what I will do: I’ll have the use of your right arm, your memory and I will come back in 15 years for your soul.”

As I expected to die before that anyway and was desperate for money and not wanting to go on the rigs I said yes. The coldness left and I went to sleep. The next day I went off to work as normal I can’t remember the exact date but think it was sometime in December, 1972.

While I was waiting to get the work on the oil rigs I still needed more money, so I applied for a better paying job, still topping trees but for a company in Godalming which was about 20 miles away. The car I had was expensive to run so I decided to go back to a motorbike and bought a 650cc Bonneville which was one of the bigger bikes at that time. I didn't tell the insurance company I had any endorsements on my licence.

On Friday, 5th January, 1973 I was finishing my job to start the new one in Godalming on the Monday. As it was my last night I offered to give a bloke called Clive a lift home. The government were just making the wearing of helmets compulsory by law so along with the bike I had bought a brand new helmet but not a full face helmet like they are today. I think my passenger had a helmet on as well. I was quite near his home when I went to overtake a car just before a dual carriageway. A car was coming towards us. As it came out into the middle of the road the front right-hand wing hit Clive's right knee. He went over the car and landed in the ditch on the other side of the road with his knee sticking out through his jeans. Meanwhile I took the driver's side door pillar out with my head. The helmet had cracked from front to back. My body bounced off the car into the side of the car I was overtaking; when I bounced off that car I ended up in the middle of the road laying across the white lines at the end of a duel carriageway. The cars and a bus pulled up on the end of the dual carriageway. At this point you need to remember the deal.

A Mark 3 Ford Zodiac passed the cars and the bus that had stopped. The driver thought I was a bundle of rags in the road and went straight across my right elbow across my body snapping my pelvis in two which ripped through my bladder. Starting from the top I was unconscious, I had fractured my skull, my brain had swelled causing epileptic fits, my cracked helmet had opened my head over my eyes. My nose was broken, my front tooth was knocked out when I had bounced along the road on my face, and one eye was swollen. It was a wonder I didn't break my neck: the fact I was quite strong must have helped. Seven ribs were broken and my lungs had collapsed. In addition to my broken pelvis and smashed bladder I had taken the skin off my knees and even the tops of my feet and a lot of my toe nails went black and fell off later. I was taken to the Royal Surrey Hospital in Guildford. I was expected to die on the first night and the police went to my parents' house to tell them that I was not expected to live and to get to the hospital as soon as they could.

My parents left the policemen in the house and came to the hospital. I was unconscious and in a bad way. The brain damage was bad and with the rest of the injuries it didn't look at all hopeful. I was on a life support machine for some time in intensive care just to keep me breathing while they decided what to do. They considered sending me to the Atkinson Morley hospital for a brain operation to relieve the pressure but because the rest of my injuries were too bad to move me, I was kept on the life support machine for two weeks and stayed unconscious for many more. They told my parents that if I survived there was a distinct possibility I'd be in a vegetative state. They had put me in a side ward even while I was unconscious and was in pain. I was fighting and my language was terrible. I don't remember coming round as such but do remember starting to become aware of drifting in and out of sleep and my parents coming to visit. One day my dad had been in to visit and I had slept right through his visit when I woke up I was very upset. I could see the top of Guilford cathedral from there with the cross on the top and started to realise the state of my body. I just wanted to die.

I had been lying on my back for about six or seven weeks I was very cold even though I had blankets and was in hospital. I was also having a battle in my spirit and my mind. As I felt cold first in my feet and then gradually up my legs, I started to think that when it got up my body to my heart I was going to die. I managed to get a nurse to 'phone my parents so I could talk to them and say goodbye. That night someone in the private ward which was next to us died and I can remember crying out to God to take me instead. I didn't want to be here. I hated disabilities and here I was: I could hardly move: I was in pain and twice a day they would drain gunge from my right elbow. I couldn't move it at all and my right hand didn't work. I couldn't move my fingers and I had epileptic seizures. I was freezing cold... and I hated myself.

I'm not sure at that time that I could remember exactly what I had done, but I cried out to God: "If you're real, help me! Could I see you?" The next thing I saw was Jesus in a white robe standing in the window, he looked at me with eyes that glowed with warmth and love - in fact his whole face shone. Nothing was said yet he spoke to me and the warmth from his face just wrapped itself around me. The next day I told the nurse that my father had visited me.

The payment

After spending nine weeks in the hospital I was allowed to go home for one week because I was so homesick, before being transferred to the Wolfsan rehabilitation hospital for a further six weeks. It was a wakeup call for me: at the time I felt very sorry for myself having to go away from home again as it reminded me of boarding school. I can remember when I arrived; having the first meal in a canteen type hall with the other people and watching people who had such bad injuries they couldn't find their mouths when they were trying to eat. I met a girl there who had been walking down the street and a vein in her head had burst causing a brain bleed that had paralysed her down one side. She showed me pictures of herself with long hair: they had shaved her to open up her head to operate. A tall man who, I was told, was a policeman from Northern Ireland; a propeller blade on a helicopter had come down and caught his head and taken a lump out of his skull so all the spare skin had been pulled together to the front. He could hardly speak or walk. Even with all the people there and the different problems to me it seemed unreal: I hoped I would wake up and find out all this was a bad dream. I can't remember how long this feeling went on for but it was a long time.

When the six weeks were up they let me back home to my parent's house. I wasn't capable of looking after myself: I was still holding my right arm up in case it fell off. I couldn't remember anything on the short term and was feeling depressed. I remembered the deal I had done with the devil and now wished I hadn't. I was on pain killers, epilepsy tablets, anti-depressant tablets.

My Dad had left the Services and taken a job with Debenhams in Guildford. He said I had to get a job and he arranged for me to have an interview in the store to work in the motor spares department. This was about September 1973 I went for the interview and bought my first ever suit and tie. When I got there the job in the spares department had gone, but they said as I had such a nice suit on they offered me a job in the menswear department instead. I knew I needed a job and I couldn't think of a way out - anyway they sent me down onto the shop floor after the basic training. The person in charge said: "Right, take this duster, go round the shirts and dust." I can remember walking around hoping that no one would walk in who I knew. I was there for about six months, suffering from depression. My joints, legs and hips all ached, especially when it got damp. I was on medication: sleeping tablets, pain killers, antidepressants and tablets to control the epilepsy. I was also banned from driving for three years so I had to walk to the train station and catch a train to Guildford.

I knew what I had done but couldn't share it with anybody because… who would believe me; that I would have been stupid enough to have done that? I can remember going back to my bedroom: Dad was at work; Mum was out. I hated myself and what I had done so I went to put Led Zeppelin's Stairway to Heaven on the record player with the cueing arm up so it would keep replaying and took a handful of sleeping tablets. I can remember lying on my bed and going to sleep… the next thing I remember is waking up in hospital after they pumped me out. Apparently I had got up, managed to stumble through the bungalow, which was quite large, and 'phoned my dad at work to say goodbye. (No mobiles then). He had 'phoned the ambulance and raced home to get me.

I was off work for some time but eventually went back to Debenhams for another few months and then got a job in a menswear boutique called Harry Fenton's in Guildford where I ended up being the manager. A young bloke came to work for me there: I can't remember his name but I can remember trying to teach him not to say, "can I help you" but to ask something else instead, to stop getting the standard response. What power is in our words! We can bless or we can curse; bring life or death. He found it very difficult but I wouldn't let up. He went off for the weekend and when he came back in he had a bandage on his hand. When I asked him what had happened he said he had an accident with a lawnmower and cut half his finger off so I renamed him Arfer (half a finger). He left a week or so after that, went into his parents garage and hanged himself.

If you have never been depressed, it must be difficult to understand; but again this black cloud of depression came over me. I was on speed to keep me up, sleeping tablets to get me to sleep, and tablets for the pain in my legs and hips - all from the doctor. I wanted to get back into the flat I'd had before the accident, the one that belonged to my parents. I thought it would give me and them some freedom if I could move back, but a man was renting it: I willed him to go. He fell down the stairs and hit his head on the boiler at the bottom of the stairs and died.

I persuaded my parents to rent me their flat again; I was still very depressed and I took another overdose. When I woke up I was in hospital again. The staff had pumped me out and a very nice black doctor with a very quiet calm voice was asking me to sign a form and come with him. At the time I remember thinking: "Is God a black man?" It makes me laugh now after seeing the film Heaven Almighty but he was just like that. I didn't sign the paper though; again I just carried on with life.

After the accident my mum got in touch with my friend Peter Pietrusiewicz, who was a policeman and a good friend, and asked him to look over the police report from the accident. Peter read it and told us that he thought we had a case as it might not have been my fault. We went to a Legal Aid solicitor and he started a case against the drivers.

It took 10 years to get heard, but just before it went to court the drivers made us an offer for £28,000 which we accepted. While this wasn't the exact amount I had agreed with the devil, I put that down to interest. During those 10 years I suffered with arthritis and rheumatism in my legs and hips. I started wearing copper bracelets and going to hypnotists to get rid of the pain; none of which worked. With the money I bought a house and just lived life. I worked as a sales rep and I still went to palmists.

A change of direction

I had always said I never wanted children or to get married as my brother has been divorced twice - and my parents ended up getting divorced, Due to my upbringing I never wanted to bring children into such a hard life and I didn't want the commitment of children or a wife. Because I didn't want a relationship to get serious I split with a girl, so a mate and I went to Majorca, to Magaluf. It was completely buzzing there, we had hardly any sleep for the first week. On the last night of my holiday I met a girl called Karen, she lived in Bromley, Kent and was still there on holiday for another week. We got together when she got back.

I was working for a company selling packaging. I also had a flat in Fleet. Later Karen moved in with me there and after a year we sold that and bought a bungalow together in Farnborough.

We wanted some fences putting up around our garden. My friend had his fence done and told me about this guy who did a really good job at a fair price. I got his number and asked him to come to give us a price for our garden fencing. He was a 6ft 8: He was an ex black belt in Karate and a bouncer in the local clubs. He stood at our doorway and I asked him how he was doing: he put his hands up and said: "I'm very well thank you, praise The Lord."

I wondered what we had on our doorstep.

My first thought was: "He is a Jehovah witness" but he was a Christian. In sales you should always focus on the lady, as they generally make the decisions, but when he was telling us about the job he focused on me. He told me about how he had fallen out with his wife and moved in to a bedsit which he shared with some Christians who always invited him to meetings. One night they told him there was food after the meeting and as he was broke he decided to go for the food. Whilst he was there, he told me, a woman had shared what had happened to her and called people who didn’t know Jesus as their personal saviour to make a commitment. He found himself walking down the aisle to the front. After that night he made a commitment to Jesus and his life had completely changed.

I asked him to give me a good price for the work, to which he answered that he would pray about what the right price should be. I told him that I would pray for a good price - which is amazing considering I didn't believe. The next day he gave me a price and I said yes, not because the price was particularly cheap but because I wanted to spend more time with him.

When he came to do the fences, I took days off work so I could find out more about him. He invited me to go to a meeting in Fleet, which was being held in a St. John’s Ambulance Hall the following Thursday night. I couldn't get it out of my mind. I spoke to Karen about going but she was not interested but she said that if I wanted to go it was up to me.

I drove up and down the street looking out at these guys standing waiting to invite people in. I waited until everyone had gone in so I could sneak in at the back. Kelvin was so pleased to see me so I sat next to him right at the back. There were about 18 others; there were girls singing with their hands up and dancing; there were no hymn books, the words were on an overhead projector. There was an old lady in a wheelchair towards the front. Someone called Jonathan started talking or preaching, I didn't know what it was at the time. He told a story and every time he spoke I got hit with waves of power that I had never experienced before. Towards the end of the meeting he said God had told him about someone's healing. They took the old lady in the wheelchair and prayed for her, then she got up and started walking around the room!

I was freaking out and kept looking at the door that was only 20 feet away. Part of me wanted to leave but I couldn't move. My head couldn't wait to get out of there but my heart felt drawn to stay. I couldn't see how someone who was in a wheelchair was now walking around the room. I thought it must have been a con, as I had a bit of money and thought they wanted it. I remembered that when I looked at the fence panels and gate, it all had his name on it. KELVIN, and every time I looked at it the letters EVIL came out at me. I had a battle in my mind; two voices: one telling me, "Get out of there!"; one telling me, "Look at what they're reading - it's the Bible. The Bible can't be evil."

Jonathan the preacher then said, as every eye was closed and every head bowed: "God told me that there are three people here who need to make a commitment tonight. This is between you, me and God, if you want to make a commitment please raise your hand, I heard him say, "thank you" once… "thank you" again… but there was no way I was raising my hand. Then Jonathan said: "God told me there is one more person that needs to make a commitment." In my head I thought: "There are only about 18 people in this meeting; you must know which ones are in. I sneaked another look at the door. There was a battle going on inside me. I could remember thinking there was no way I was getting into this on my first night but my heart still felt drawn to it. Then he said these words: "I take authority over you, Satan and you are bound in this place, in the name of Jesus."

As he said that I felt my hand go up, and I heard him say, "thank you", and I put my hand down as quickly as I could, thinking: "Oh no! What have I done?" and I heard this voice saying: "I have got you, you know." I thought I had signed up with the devil but I knew I hadn't. I thanked Kelvin and was just about to go when the preacher came up, introduced himself as Pastor Jon Fiddy and asked if he could pray for me. He lead me in a prayer:

"Father, I come to you in Jesus' name. I acknowledge that I am a sinner, and I ask you to forgive my sins and wash me clean with your precious blood. I believe in Jesus, that he is the son of God and rose from the dead. I receive you Lord into my life as my Lord and my saviour. Please lead me from this time onward. Amen."

I thanked him and left as quickly as I could. As I sat in my car I cried my eyes out. I couldn't drive as I couldn't see through the tears. When I got back home I knew I was different. I still smoked, my body was the same, but I was changed inside. I couldn't explain how I was different, I just knew I was different. Karen wasn't sure what had happened to me but I believe she knew something was different.

The prayer had changed the direction of my life. I didn't realise it then but my desires started to be different. I was smoking between 30 or 40 a day which in a way I wanted to give up. It took me and Karen over a year to stop, then God took it away for both of us on the same night and I've not touched a cigarette since then. In fact I'm an avid non smoker now and have been for over 30 years.

I was working for a company selling glass washing machines and commercial catering equipment to pubs clubs and hotels. As part of my job I would go around calling on pubs and over the next few weeks, I was being really blessed. As I was calling, people started being pleased to see me, I seemed to be in the right place at the right time and was getting orders coming to me. I felt different, cut down on my swearing and tried my best not to tell lies. One time I was in a pub selling and the installation manager Paul called me, I lied to him over the phone. It was really strange: I heard this voice inside me say you shouldn't have done that. We worked in an open plan office. The people in the office already thought I had changed and was strange because most people in the office swore, and Paul, who was in charge, used to give it large to his blokes as he ran the installation and service side. Anyway, I was convicted that I should say sorry to Paul for lying to him and ask his forgiveness. I thought: "Man, this is hard." I went back to the office, walked upstairs into our open plan office and walked up to him. Inside I could hear him laughing and all the people in the office, however when I told him I was sorry for lying to him and asked him to forgive me, he just said: "Thanks, that's okay." It's surprising when we do what we are directed to do we have an inner strength.

---

*Abba means 'Father' in Aramaic. It's the word Jesus used to refer to his Father God.

Abba*

I had arranged to marry Karen long before either of us had become Christians. At first I didn't like the idea of having children: I'd seen my parents' divorce and my older brother Vincent went on to divorce twice. I just didn't expect marriages to last very long, so why bring children into the situation? I still loved Karen though and as we'd become Christians some attitudes still needed correcting in me. What most people don't realise is that when you get born again all things change in your heart, but there are years of bad habits and ideas that need sorting. God will change them if you're willing. As the Bible says, we work out our salvation in fear and trembling. That's when stubborn ideas change - sometimes without you even realising.

So, I'd arranged with Karen to get married and then we both became Christians and, as everything was arranged, we tied the knot the very same year. The Registry Office in Woking had already been booked and funnily enough it also coincided with Karen's birthday.

We had our reception at "Mr Bumble" in Camberley, run by a guy named Dave. I'd sold this pub a lot of catering equipment so we knew each other and had a really good time at the reception.

I wanted to know more about this Bible and about this Jesus. Someone bought me a Good News Bible. I went home and even had a battle to open and read it. I opened it in the middle, thinking half would be the Old Testament and half would be the New Testament. It wasn't, so I left it until Karen got home and she showed me. I used to go to the Waterman's Art Centre for a coffee and a cigarette and started taking my Bible to read even though I didn't really understand a lot of what I was reading but was just excited. A guy who worked there, who I used to talk to, came over and asked me why I was reading the Bible. I told him I'd been to a meeting and become a Christian and he said: "What kind of Christian are you?" I said: "I don't know" and told him what had happened to me: he was shocked.

I was fairly sure that my boss had taken my Bible from the back of my company car which he had the keys for. He wouldn't admit that he'd had taken it. When I got into the car I was so angry that I reversed too quickly, hit a post and damaged the car quite badly.

Kelvin had been coming around the house when he could, which was very helpful. I used to swear quite badly but Kelvin showed me in the Bible in James chapter 3, verses 3-12 that blessings and curses shouldn't both come out of your mouth. It's difficult to start with, but if you want to do something and you're determined enough and ask the Holy Spirit for help he will help you. The way you find out how you're doing with this is the time you hit your finger with a hammer or similar. What's the first thing that comes out of your mouth?

I decided to read the 10 Commandments and to see what I scored. Exodus chapter 20 verse 1 to 17 lists the 10 Commandments. I read them and thought wryly I'd done quite well: I'd broken nine out of ten. I clearly heard God say: "No you haven't, you've done all ten."

"Hang on," I replied. "I've admitted to nine but I've not murdered anyone. Nothing more was said to me.

My ex-girlfriend and fiancée was called Sharon. A couple of weeks later I visited her mother because I had an appointment near where she lived. She was a Welsh lady. When she answered the door, however, she was very upset with me about her daughter. Sharon, who was now married, was in the new Guildford Hospital with Crohn's disease. She was waiting to have her womb removed and had told her mother that she and I had decided for her to have an abortion some years earlier. When they did the abortion she was having twins. When I left there I didn't know what to do so I parked down the road and cried out to God.

As I was crying out to God, I came out with the word 'Abba.' I spoke it out but it didn't mean anything to me. I thought 'Abba.' I said it again. The only ABBA I could think was the group from Sweden. I cried out to God again asking him what I should do: the next word out of my mouth was 'Jonathan.' I thought that was the pastor from the meeting I went to and I knew he believed in healing. I knew that Sharon was in the new Guildford Hospital but I didn't know her surname now she was married. I 'phoned Jonathan and asked if he would be prepared to come to the hospital and pray for her. He said he needed to pray about it, and would I phone him later? I didn't want him to pray, just to say yes so we could get on with it. I made my way over to the new hospital and 'phoned Jon again. This time he said yes, he could come with me tomorrow.

I described to the staff on the reception desk what was wrong with Sharon and found out which ward she was on. When I went up to the ward I found her lying in bed, not looking at all well, and her husband was sitting there. He was not pleased to see me. I explained that I was now a Christian and that I'd met this pastor who was prepared to come over the next day to pray for her and told them he seemed to have a healing ministry. They agreed but I had to promise him that I wouldn't ever get in touch with her again after that. I arranged to pick up the pastor the next day, after giving the car a hoover and clean because it smelt of cigarettes.

When we arrived at the hospital the following day I was very nervous about what was going to happen; what her husband would say if he was there and whether we would be able to pray in the hospital. Anyway, we got to the nurses station - I think it was on the fifth floor - and just said we had come to see Sharon. The ward only had about eight beds and hers was near the window. Her husband was sitting there but when we walked in he got up and walked out without saying a word. I introduced Jon to her: we chatted for a minute or two and it was clear she was in a bad way. Jon explained that we all need to be born again and get right with God. He then asked if he could pray with her and after some hesitation she said yes. I was standing there thinking: "We are not far from the nurse's station" - and there were nurses there but it was like the people didn't notice us at all. Jon told me to pull the curtains round. He asked her if could pray for her and did she know she was a sinner? She said she wasn't, which is how most of us feel. But you can't rely on your feelings. He explained that we are all sinners and need the forgiveness of God. He prayed for her to receive Jesus as her Lord and Saviour. Then he started to pray for her healing and that they wouldn't cut her womb out. He bound the works of the devil in her life and the Crohn's disease. By now he was shouting. I was just standing at the opening of the curtains looking inside at Jon and then looking at the nurse's station. I could barely believe what was going on because the people were looking but didn't move as if we weren't there. When he had finished she was spark out on the bed. I suddenly saw paper headlines flash across in front of me saying 'Man prays for woman in hospital and she passes out.' Jon brought her round and I pulled the curtain back. Saying "thank you," we walked out - no one else said anything: we got down to the car and I drove the pastor home.

I kept my word and have never been directly in touch with her since that day, but I do know they cancelled the operation and I'm sure she has at least two children.

I felt God say to me: "I told you that you had broken all ten of my commandments." I now felt very convicted that I had even broken the commandment not to murder. If that's correct that means it's not about the amount of weeks someone is pregnant: the baby inside the womb is a person. I believe it's a trick of Satan which means we sacrifice millions of souls every year in the name of free choice. If you have done this, at the end of this book there is a prayer you can pray to release yourself from the guilt of what you have done. I believe our God doesn't want you carrying this or any other burden. In the Bible God says his yoke is easy and his burden is light (Matthew chapter 11, verse 30).

This is for Christians too. I've met so many Christians who aren't smiling because they are carrying a heavy burden. God sent Jesus to turn us around and to set us free. If at this point you feel condemned, please don't! When God convicts us of the things we have done wrong he always shows us a way out. When the devil condemns us he drives us into situations that make us feel that there is no way out. God draws us and wants us to have freedom to serve him. The devil drives us and says it's all our fault: that's one of his tactics. We are living in a sin-sick, fallen world. If you want to get out of the situation you find yourself in you need to pray a prayer of repentance which means to be sorry with sincere regret for all you have done wrong. You need to believe that Jesus is the son of God and ask him into your heart.

Picture this, it's amazing… When God designed and made us, he put a door to our hearts by which he can enter in to us but he didn't put a handle on the outside. Which means the only way for him to enter our hearts is for us to open that door from the inside and ask him in. He won't force his way into your heart.

It also amazes me that the God who spoke everything into being has given humans free will to decide if we will open our hearts to him. This is what we all need to do to enter into a relationship with the King of kings and Lord of lords. There are lots of gods out there: people make their own gods; gods they are comfortable with; gods that don't really challenge them. You can serve a god and not realise it.

Lots of people follow football teams or motor racing. If you have ever watched a football match you'll know that when a goal is scored or someone gets fouled, people in the crowd raise their arms and start cheering and singing. They do that because that's the team that they're supporting - or if they are opposed to them they are on their feet to complain. That's completely normal, but somehow we're viewed as fanatics at church when we lift our hands. It’s part of us surrendering and lifting up the name of our God.

What I liked about going around with Jonathan; wherever he went there was something happening. I used to go and see him for prayer and deliverance. He prayed for a lot of things and delivered me from a number of demons. One day he was praying for my right arm and my elbow. As he did that I felt the skin on my elbow lift up as something came out from within my scar. Another time he was praying for my head and my mind and my brain damage and he was telling this demon to come out of my head: I used to get terrible headaches. Suddenly I heard a voice inside of my head saying: “Stop him now! Stop him now!” - which I ignored - and Jon kept on telling this demon to come out. This voice said to me: “Stop him now or I’m bringing your brain out through the top of your head.” I told Jon to stop but didn’t tell him why straight away because I was afraid. I think lots of people don’t like themselves, what they’re into or what they’ve done but they don’t know what to do, or they think there’s no escape.

He prayed for my legs. I used to get terrible arthritis. When he prayed it was another strange one: as he was praying I was sitting there and my legs felt very strange. As he prayed my feet became black as I looked at them. Something seemed to be coming out of them and this shadow became twice as long as my feet. I don’t know what it was but it left that day and never came back.

Later on, one Sunday evening, there was an outreach and healing meeting in the local hall that Jon had hired. I was still a smoker then so I used to have a quick cigarette before I went in and this evening I was late. I was still having problems with headaches and pains in my head. When I walked into the meeting Jon had just started praying with people. As I walked up for prayer and got near to Jon something hit me in the chest and knocked me backwards straight through rows of chairs. I landed next to two people who looked horrified. Apparently this was the first time they had ever been to a Christian meeting!

Pastor Jonathan Fiddy

There is power in the God we serve: this is not about religion, it's about relationship. If there is no power, God is not taking part. Our God is the God of power. I see in the church today that people are telling God what to do instead of asking God what he wants us to do. God said my sheep hear my voice (John, chapter 10, verse 27). So, as sheep we should follow the good shepherd because our God loves everyone so much that he was prepared to give his only son that he might go to the cross for all our sin sickness that we have already gone through and all that we will go through. We all need to be born again. Because Jesus is alive. He is knocking at the door of your heart waiting for you to let him in. God says now is the time of salvation. Don't put it off and think it's all right for old fogeys: it clearly says that no one knows the day or the hour the Lord's going to return. And you don't know when God is calling you back - you might be ultra-fit.

When I was 17 or 18 I went to get my palms and cards read but I want to tell you that you might get 95% truth but the 5% that's lies means that you'll miss the mark by miles. If you're not getting your information from God and his Holy Spirit, you're getting it from another source. Jon used to have midweek evening prayer meeting: I felt I wanted to go but I was still having a battle. I used to go to the flat where they met and stand outside; I couldn't knock on the door. I tried to work this out, it went on for ages: I would give up, sit in the car and then drive home.

The blessing of children

Now although at first I didn't want kids, we had started to plan a family. But Karen couldn't get pregnant. After seven years of trying we really worried that we'd got a problem. Medical tests showed no abnormalities but still nothing was happening. It affected Karen who was getting frustrated seeing others start their families. Various people, some of them preachers, had prayed for us. We trusted God could move, but after so much time we wondered if our dream of having a child had completely gone. After all, Karen wasn't getting any younger and age is a factor in whether you get a heathy child or not. It was a constant concern but an unintentional meeting led our circumstances to change.

Jon had heard about a preacher from New Zealand who was preaching over here and had a spare evening which we could put him on in Fleet. Jon was very excited about this and invited six to eight of us to meet up to discuss a strategy. I went to this meeting not knowing what I could do to help but was excited. There was an editor of a magazine, other people who were mature Christians and me. Jon told us all he needed in the way of help; the different areas he needed covering: prayer people, stewards, councillors, book and cassette sales. The event also needed leaflets and advertising - getting in touch with the local papers, radio stations. He asked us to pray and then went around asking each person what they wanted to get involved in, if anything. As I was sitting there I felt the only thing I could offer would be the advertising, even though I knew very little about it but there was a man sitting there who was involved with newspapers! When Jon asked him he said something else, so when it got to me I knew I should volunteer.

The New Zealand preacher was called Barry Smith. He and his wife May were going to stay with someone else while we were hosting his son Andrew, together with his wife and baby. When they arrived Andrew and his wife Saskia were not very well, so Barry and May decided they wanted to come and stay with them. We then had a full house but it was the start of a wonderful friendship.

Barry Smith was a Christian preacher, Bible teacher and author, who had written books on Bible prophecy and was travelling extensively, evangelising throughout the world, speaking about the end times in relation to Bible prophecy and current world events.

He was a jolly man; we immediately took to him for his friendliness, great fun and serious Christian faith. He could make you laugh and yet get you to understand Bible texts easily. Meeting him for the first time he showed us his “Daily Light” scripture readings.

We had hired the local town centre hall which would hold about 400 on the night.

Over 450 people were packed into the hall. Some were sitting on the stage and I was standing in the foyer with quite a few people who couldn’t get in. When he had finished preaching, Barry got the musicians to play Amazing Grace and told people if they wanted to make a decision to follow Christ that they should come forward to the stage - and he would pray for them to become born again and change their destiny.

Barry preached for about two hours. It was intense, funny, it was real. It was about the coming one-world system the one-world church, the rise of the antichrist and the mark of the beast. It was about the return of Jesus to come back for his own who were sinners redeemed by the blood of the lamb; The ones who are looking for him, waiting for him. I was blown away by the number of people who were there: they had listened for over two hours, they had laughed, they had heard they needed to do something to be free from their sin and experience rebirth; to step out of darkness into his glorious light. It was amazing: as the musicians played, people were coming out of their seats into the middle aisle and starting to walk forward. As I said, I was right at the back in the foyer. A woman standing near me came over and said she wanted to go forward but she was a Catholic. I said I didn't think that should stop her and said I'd walk down with her. As I was walking forward there were lots of people standing in the aisle not sure what to do. I was collecting people as I went forward. When we all got to the front Barry prayed for them and we took as many names and 'phone numbers as we could, so we could follow up afterwards. It was the first of many awesome meetings we had over the next ten years.

A few years later following another successful tour of the UK Barry and May stayed with us, during their last evening Barry offered to lay hands on us, which they did, and prayed that we should bear children to the glory of the Lord.

Barry prayed that we may have the same blessing as Sarah, and I thought, "Oh yeah – right!" which meant I hadn't much faith that it would ever happen for us.

You know God has faith when we don't - because about a month later Karen said she was pregnant! We called our first child Becky. After all those years it actually happened and we were so pleased and thankful that at last our prayers and others' prayers on our behalf had all been answered. God's timing is perfect and Barry came into our lives at the correct time. He had made a big impression on us and we decided to go to New Zealand at the invitation of Barry and May where we went to a wedding. Karen was three months pregnant at the time! Our second child we named Jordan! Praise God – for he is good!

We were privileged to look after Barry and May many times as they would stay with us most times when they were over here. Together with Jon and Debbie and another couple called John and Joan we worked together to arrange the tours. We would get many invites from people and churches who wanted to host the meetings. So we decided we would go down to visit the places we had been invited to help people with the things they needed to do and about the costs and the offerings. We never charged an entrance fee because the Bible says, "freely you have received; freely give." (Mathew chapter 10, verses 5 to 8). Normally Barry spoke for three nights and would share for over two hours each night. It was always followed by a call for people to come forward if they wanted to give their lives over to Jesus. I loved to get on the stage just behind Barry to oversee everything that was going on and to watch the people come forward to receive Jesus. I have seen many people making their way forward over the years. One of my favourite meetings was in London. While the musicians played Amazing Grace, as they did every time we finished the meetings, Barry called the people forward to start a new life, turning away from everything they knew to be wrong and asking Jesus to forgive them.

Jesus says he stands at the door of your heart and knocks.

What a fantastic thing to be able to walk away from everything you've done wrong; all the wrong decisions; all the wrong actions; all the wrong thoughts! God says in his Word that you do sin, even in thought, not just action. This is why no one can stand before God and say, "I've not sinned" because the Bible covers that one: it says that all have sinned and fallen short. It is only by grace you can be saved, not by works, so no one can boast. That means you can be the best person, but still need to be born again because that's what gets you into heaven. And you still won't be able to boast that you deserve to be there! In fact when you have this experience - which is to be truly born - suddenly you know you're different and everything has changed.

We were involved with Barry Smith for a long time and brought him and May to England. Going back to the early days, we were contacted by a cameraman called Howard Condor who was working out of his home in Kingston. He came down and filmed Barry's meeting so we had videos we could sell as well as some books Barry had written. Howard went on to start and run Revelation TV.

Karen and I went on holiday, camping in France with Jon and Debbie and their children Tash and Josh. They used to share their children with us as we seemed unable to have our own. On the way back the crossing was terrible and when we got off the ferry we all said: "thank goodness that's over!" and "We won't do that again in a hurry." We got back to Fleet and Jon had a call from a person in the Isle of Wight who ran Barry's ministry saying he couldn't do it anymore and if we wanted to take over running the ministry we needed to go over to the Isle of Wight that day to pick everything up! We hired a van and had to go straight back on a ferry to pick all the stuff up from him. Hasn't God got a sense of humour? He knows the beginning from the end.

We were blessed a third time with a child, Grace, and so completed our family. Prayers had been answered in ways which neither Barry nor we could have imagined. I'd changed as well, I loved having my children, getting involved at every stage in their growing years. I even did nappies and feeding, God had done a great work in transforming me.
We are so blessed to have been part of Barry's ministry, sadly he died in 2002. His son wrote of him:

> "Many, many people either became Christians or were encouraged… because of this man sowing seeds in their lives, and the harvest continues on. He travelled by invitation only, often packing out large churches, auditoriums and even stadiums – his messages and views were entertaining, compelling and sometimes controversial. Literally thousands of people committed their lives to Jesus Christ following Barry's preaching."

It's not about playing harps

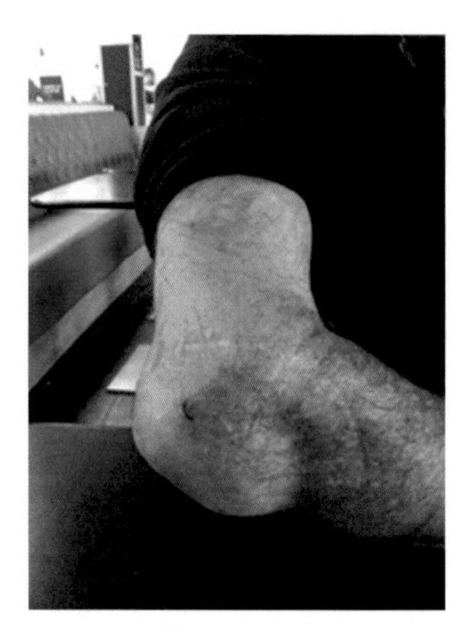

Since my accident, as I have no right elbow joint, if I hit my elbow my right hand stops working and I get terrible pains run down my arm into my fingers. My short term memory is not good because of the brain damage I had. What I've found over the years however is that you find ways to overcome these problems. I really struggled in the early days: I carried my arm like it was going to fall off.

Before I became a Christian I used to get extremely depressed. I took two overdoses because I hated myself, what I'd done and the consequences. But I didn't want to go to hell. I have spoken to many people over the years: some think hell's going to be great - they think it's going to be partying. That's because heaven is sold so short, as if you're going to be sitting on a cloud somewhere playing a harp - that sounds truly boring. There's nothing wrong with people who play harps, but I really want you to know the truth. The truth will set you free. (John, chapter 8, verses 31-32). (Revelation 20, verse 6) says we will reign with Christ. The Word tells us that "blessed and holy is he who has part in the first resurrection. Over such, the second death has no power, but they shall be priests of God and of Christ, and shall reign with him a thousand years." This is not harp playing as I see it.

Talking to people and encouraging them over the past years has been a great honour and privilege; to think the God of the universe has allowed me to be used to speak into people's lives. The limits to what we can do in God's strength is only down to us: we can have the best gifts and, as a very good friend says, the gifts can get you to places that your character won't keep you. That's profound. Let God lead you and take you on an exciting journey. Another good friend of mine says: "Things happen in my life, not all good, but things happen."

I think it's good to give thanks in all situations but not to 'rest on our laurels'. I would hate to be totally comfortable because God says we are in the world but not of the world (John, chapter 17 verses 15-19). Therefore our permanent home is not here; it is somewhere else and when we get there we can rest. If we try to work everything out so we understand it, we will miss most of what God has got for us, because God works by faith. He wants us to step out of the natural and move into the supernatural.

When Howard was trying to set up a television station in Spain he came against lots of opposition. In the natural way of doing things there was no way forward: he had gone out there as a ground breaker, which is always very hard. I used to speak to him to encourage him. One day I was thinking about him and suddenly saw him standing before a large mirror in a bathroom and he was saying to the Lord there is no way forward and he was ready to give up. As I watched, God told me: "This is his choice now he can stay where he is or he can walk with me in the supernatural." Then I saw him taking a step forward, through the mirror, into his destiny. This is the difference between the natural and the supernatural. Where do you want to be? You can be safe in the natural, which reminds me of the

Parable of the Talents (Mathew, chapter 25, verses14-30) which is about the different attitudes people have. I believe that God created us all and is calling us all. He is establishing his people who love him and want to serve him, for the glory of his kingdom. In the Lord's Prayer we say:

Our Father who is in heaven,
hallowed be your name,
Your kingdom come
Your will be done on earth as it is in heaven.
Give us this day our daily bread
and forgive us our trespasses as we forgive those who trespass against us
and lead us not into temptation
but deliver us from the evil
for thine is the Kingdom, the power and the glory, for ever and ever

Mathew, chapter 6 verses 9-15

If you read this prayer I suggest you read it line by line and ask God to give you an understanding of it he will do.

The reason for writing this is to share some of my experiences; to show that there is another way to go that will wipe out all the past; all the things you have done wrong. Some of these you will know about, but some you don't even realise you've done. So I suggest you pray the 'Prayer of Salvation', get rid of everything in the past and start again: watch God move in you. The process of cleansing has to start inside you. Apparently when communism started it promised to put a new suit on every man. God puts a new person in every suit - or dress! I thank you for taking the time to read this. Please pray the prayer at the end of this, if you mean it from your heart, I believe. it will change you into the person God wants you to be. We are living in the last days. I believe we will see Jesus return in our lifetime for those who know him and are looking forward to his return. It says in Luke, chapter 21, verse 28: "Look up, for your redemption draws near." Pray the 'Prayer of Salvation', then tell a friend and find a good church that believes that the Bible is the written word of God. Get involved, give your time, but don't be used by anyone who wants to take advantage of you. God loves you for who you are but we all need to be changed to become more like Jesus. God will do that by his Holy Spirit. Make sure the church leader is born again, Spirit filled and living for God.

Father, I come to you in Jesus' name.

I acknowledge that I am a sinner, and I ask you to forgive my sins and wash me clean with your precious blood.

I believe in Jesus, that he is the son of God and rose from the dead.

I receive you Lord into my life as my Lord and my saviour. Please lead me from this time onward.

Amen.

My name is Steve Avery. My email address is s-avery1@sky.com . If you've prayed this prayer for the first time, please let me know. God bless you and I pray that God will make his face to shine on you.

Steve Avery
Photo: Martin Lonsdale

Ray's Story

My story is an on-going advent. The Holy spirit doesn't just stop with one, he works through and with them and changes their lives. Here is one testimony amongst many others, but this is one of the more dramatic one's, that could of have been convinced by the Lord himself.

Ray Crossman and the interaction with Steve Avery

1993 was a strange year, I was selling Double Glazing, Conservatories, Facias Soffits and Guttering for a small but growing company in Basingstoke called 'Brackenwood Windows Ltd'.

This was a 'commission only' sales position, so as a salesman if you didn't sell then you earned nothing at all, so it was important to me to be somewhat excellent at everything I did so that at the very least I could support my family. We'd just come out of a bad economic recession and people were becoming more confident about spending money again and improving their homes.

Then came a small influx of other salesmen, and the company had rented a shop and had it converted to a showroom at a place called Frimley Green near Farnborough.

This was also coincidental when some of my colleagues said that some religious nutter, someone behaving like a Jehovah's Witness, had joined as a salesman and was taking over the new showroom and his name was Steve Avery.

Well, that didn't mean much to me, and as a confident man of thirty-six years old and a freemason who had just reached 'master mason', felt that there was no threat to my standing.

Unfortunately, life sometimes takes an awkward turn, and it had for me. My brother (sibling) had been having psychotic events after an operation following a serious hang glider flying accident. His behavioral episodes were alarming, the fear, the imaginary threats and the paranoia he was experiencing were ongoing. Pills and talking him through his worries seemed to be having no benefit and his paranoia was getting worse.

I felt responsible for my brother, but also to my family with two young sons and a wife to support, I needed to be self-confident, to succeed - all of which was in my own strength.

Freemasonry was supposed to be an improvement course along which a man rose by degrees ever learning more 'secrets' and becoming 'perfected'. Socially it was fun, yet serious in nature, the bonding between the men (the brothers) was satisfying and the confidence one got from speaking in front of many men boosted one's ego. It was a 'craft' my father once told me to join if ever I got the chance and 'following the traditions of men' I did so, all be it nervously and with a number of questions and suspicions of my own.

I had been in the 'craft' three years prior to my encounter with Steve Avery and I had a number of reservations by then about what I had become involved in. Nevertheless the 'ceremonies', the mixing with colleagues, the annual ladies' nights and the massaging of the ego after every masonic session, masked my doubts about freemasonry.

Strangely I became inquisitive about some of the biblical references upon which some of these ceremonies were based. They predominately focused on Old Testament stories of King Soloman's temple, used names of people who were eminent in many of those old stories. It was if they had been borrowed and added to for masonic credibility, for when one looked up the references in the bible, these masonic connections appeared to have been embellished.

Given freemasonry was said to not be a religion, it seemed odd that the Old Testament featured highly and also prayers were offered up in the lodge to the 'Great Architect' in what was a building represented as that reflecting the workings of King Soloman's temple!

So, this was the background to my life and then meeting Steve was an interesting encounter. My first thoughts were how did he become so physically injured, why was he so keen to talk about Jesus? Perhaps his church was short of members, perhaps he had some sort of brain damage that caused him to fantasize, it could be that he was just a religious nut out to discredit people who hadn't got his beliefs. Whatever the reason, I was too busy really to interact with Steve, for I had sales to get, journeys to make to visit and support my brother who was in mental turmoil.

My brother was getting increasingly worse despite tablets, visits to the doctor and having every assistance from my sister and myself. My suspicions about freemasonry were also growing, for I witnessed some of the men there becoming increasingly egocentric, argumentative and intransigent in some of their pathetic ideas. For those who used to watch the comings and goings of 'Dad's Army' on TV would be just as amused about some of the silly carryings on in the lodge.

I was never feeling desperate in all these difficulties but was operating very much in my own strength trying to help my brother, earn enough to get by, travelling many miles giving people quotes, but given my sense of urgency this resulted in increased sales.

Meeting Steve again was at one of our sales meetings, he was made fun of by some of the salesmen, which he didn't seem to mind. I remember though he seemed to have an interest in me, and I wasn't ready to involve myself in any religiosity – my interests were as you can imagine elsewhere. I listened politely to what he had to say, didn't really take much notice and went on my way.

I think I heard from some of the other sales people that Steve was running the sales office in Frimley Green and they used to say that he being religious - was running a 'charity shop' as they called it. Always up for a laugh, it became known as the 'charity shop' which on reflection was really rather unkind.

We probably met a number of times and Steve always slid in some Christian slant to his conversation which for the most part got ignored. He spoke about his church and those miraculous things that happened there, that there was something called 'end times', something about a bloke called Barry Smith – much of which seemed like fiction from another planet.

But there was one occasion where Steve started his usual Christian dialogue which filled me with utter rage. He must have known I was involved with freemasonry because he said, your good works won't save you, for it says in the Bible that 'your good works are but filthy rags to God'. "How dare you" I said and I had every intention of checking these words out to see that they were untrue. On the next occasion I saw Steve I marched up to him and in a fit of indignation expressed that Steve should keep quiet, stop trying to evangelize people and stop upsetting them. Boy, was I mad with him, but my motivation was not premeditated or thought out, it just exploded outwards from deep within me and poor Steve must have wondered what had been thrust upon him.

Though I was now relieved to have said my piece, I still wasn't satisfied and so looked up what had been said by Steve and true enough it says in the scriptures that 'your good works are but filthy rags to God'!

Isaiah 64:6

Now this contradicted everything I understood to be admired in a person and certainly good works were always an attribute of freemasonry. Good works require effort, cost and sacrifice so why such an alarmist statement? I was searching the scriptures in the Old Testament anyway and reading some anti-masonic books as well to try and understand what was wrong with freemasonry. My doubts were growing particularly when there was an announcement in the lodge about charity medals being issued according to what one gives in response to the Grand Master of Berkshire's charity of the year.

If you gave £100 you got a bronze medal, £200 got you a silver medal and if you gave £500 you got a gold medal to wear on your lapel whilst in the lodge. Do you know some men walked around with so many of these medals you'd think they had been decorated in war service as they clanked along.

This clearly was another nail in the coffin of masonic reputation for me for I knew that charity should be given without any form of applause or fanfare. But as I found out, charity is applauded, advertised and heralded as a masonic virtue – for the benefit of the masonic egos of course.

The bible says something about when you give do not let the left hand know what the right hand is doing, in other words don't brag about your giving – there shouldn't be any egocentric personal benefit in it.

My brother wasn't improving, his paranoia getting ever worse and despite all the usual family efforts this looked like a losing battle. Suicide had been mentioned but we never thought that would ever happen, but the sadness, anxiety that was gripping my brother was alarming to witness.

Then Steve happened to come into the office, and asked how things were and I opened up about this desperate situation with my brother's mental health. He asked me something like 'would you like us to pray for him'? Believing that I thought Steve was going away and do some nice prayers at his church with his fellow Christians, I said yes that would be nice. But instead, he said, ok let's pray now and he started to pray to Jesus presenting a case for protection and healing for my brother.

Locked in a mutual handshake I agreed on what prayer requests Steve was making and I remember feeling something in my heart. I felt that there was a compassion in Steve, but also that he really believed in Jesus as a person to whom the prayer requests he was making. Not only that but Steve was full of belief and faith, that these would be answered.

This wasn't just theory or head knowledge; it was something of a deeply held conviction that Steve had and the moment touched me inside. It was in that moment, I knew that Steve had something to offer, and it wasn't just egotistical ideas, it was something much deeper and unlike a religious zealot, his faith was real and caring.

Over the next weeks my brother went missing, he'd fled from his flat – whereabouts unknown. Whilst he sounded suicidal, stricken with fear, paranoia and depression, I never thought he'd do the ultimate act, but not knowing where he was, added to my and my family's anxiety.

Somehow, I met Steve's wife Karen, who had heard of my dilemma, possibly through Steve and she said that they'd be praying for my brother, which in itself demonstrated a genuine concern from people I hardly knew.

Over the weeks my brother still remained missing, my sister ended up on TV's missing persons helpline programme, begging for someone to report his whereabouts. Freemasonry still had it's quirky behaviour, and my encounter with Steve was enflaming my spiritual curiosity.

On another encounter with Steve, I asked him about his life, the church he attended, what was all this stuff about the Holy Spirit, miracles and Jesus. Humbly he explained what he knew, and you could tell that he fervently believed and wanted others to be satisfied with the Christian faith as well.

It hadn't affected him that many including myself, had mocked him, a further reason to take him more seriously.

The transformation begins.

Then, out of the blue he asked if I'd like to go on the Wednesday night to the Harlington Centre in Fleet, where his church was putting on an event called a 'Testimony Night'.

I agreed and knowing that many Christians were going to give an account of their faith, I was interested to find out what was behind this transformation of people.

I arrived at this community centre well ahead of time, was greeted at the door by Steve and there was another person whom I knew, so I was not entirely a stranger. I remember there was a small worship team of singers and in amongst them was Karen, Steve's wife. What amazed me was not only were they singing Christian songs that I had never heard of, but when they sang - they weren't just expelling words and sounds, they looked like they believed in every word they sang!

One of the tunes was 'God will find a way – where there seems to be no way' - and it resonated in my heart and the stage was set for an interesting evening.

After the worship time a few prayers were offered up in the name of Jesus and the meeting was opened and individuals were sequentially invited onto the stage to give their accounts of how they became Christians. What amazed me was that they talked about 'being born again' - something Steve had mentioned to me previously, a concept that seemed alien to me but universal to all these folk.

Time after time each individual spoke of transformation, leaving old habits, healings, life changes, optimism for the future, breaking with bad relationships, taking up regular church attendance, thankfulness to Jesus and obedience under the power of the Holy Spirit.

As I sat there listening to one after the other, I thought a couple of profound things.

Firstly, these folk were all of different backgrounds, education, life experiences, ages, sexes, aspirations in life and Holy Spirit experiences. Dare I say it they were all of different classes, income levels, employment status's and yet they were brought together as one group with the same core belief in Jesus as their personal saviour.

Secondly these weren't gullible people, easily swayed by some intricate propaganda and exuberant preaching – they must have been convinced by some simple message and by something rather powerful. Little did I know I'd discover my conclusions would have a confirmation in a dramatic way.

<u>The Holy Spirit Encounter.</u>

By now I was ready to receive any help I could with my brother still missing and finally finding after many weeks his car abandoned in a Basingstoke shopping centre car park.

Steve said his church would continue praying for a good outcome and then asked me to come along to another meeting at the Harlington – this time their preacher 'Jonathan Fiddy' would be preaching and that they expected signs and wonders following – a terminology of which I knew nothing.

Pastor Jonathan Fiddy is a quiet unassuming character, but as he rose to his feet and began preaching his sermon about who Jesus was, how his death on the cross paid for our personal sins, his enthusiasm, quick references to the bible verses and shear energy of delivery was quite something to see. He also explained how the 'stripes' that Jesus suffered on the cross on his back were for our healing today, all of which made for an evening I'd never encountered. There was more to come as he spoke, and the air in the room changed, feeling light and what I now call the 'duvet effect'.

Jonathan asked if anyone would like prayers for healing to come forward and about ten people responded standing in a line where Steve and Jonathan began asking them for their requests and praying as the worship team sang in the background a Christian song.

He also asked those who felt touched to come to the front to receive Jesus into their hearts. Someone asked me if I'd like to go forward to which I said "no way" and remained in my seat awaiting the next episode of the evening.

I think Jonathan may have made another request and somehow, I ended up in the prayer line who by this time were being prayed for by Steve and Jonathan and mysteriously falling and being caught by catchers. They were at peace laying there on the floor as if they'd been hypnotized or so I thought.

Having known something about hypnosis, I thought well if you don't want to be hypnotized you can forcibly prevent it from happening. As each person prayed for ended up on the floor, the 'prayers' were ever coming towards me with everyone eventually laying 'slain in the spirit' falling on the floor as I now know.

Steve and Jonathan eventually arrived at me, and Jonathan asked if I'd like to receive Jesus as my Lord and Saviour, and as I'd never had anything against Jesus – I said yes.

Jonathan led me in a prayer of repentance and a prayer to receive Jesus into my heart, to which inside I had thoughts of - "This is weird, what am I doing on a Wednesday evening – now being prayed for, saying nice things, with two men laying their hands on my shoulder".

I did say the prayer faithfully and had no objection to what I was saying and just as I finished saying Amen – the effect of these two men praying for me was amazing. If you could imagine someone taking a live mains electricity lead and placing bare wires on their head, with strong vibrating electric current flowing down inside their skeleton, well that was what I experienced.

The power was so intense, but it was a rejuvenating power which overtook any control I had with my own body. Fearing I might fall I remained upright and as still as possible, barely just moving my eyeballs, but overwhelmed by this intense, rejuvenating energy which was rising and falling through my bones and not my flesh. It was amazing, better than anything I'd ever experienced, very strange but so invigorating and restoring.

Steve and Jonathan moved away from me unaware of what I was experiencing and enjoying, and though I hadn't fallen like the others, was nevertheless under the power of what I now know to be was the 'Holy Spirit'.

After what felt like ten minutes, the floor dwellers eventually arose and I gradually got the confidence to return to my chair, but the oscillating power was still flowing up and down inside me.

I had always had a right knee that ached, probably due to too much football trying to emulate Bobby Charlton's rocket shots when I was younger. After that night, pain gone, energy still flowing, and a strong feeling of rejuvenation and a cleaning process going on inside.

I don't remember how I left that meeting, but I knew that I'd changed, I was different and was and still being intensively re-energized. Driving home it must have been about 10:30pm when I arrived and in a form of desperation, I just had to tell someone about what I had seen, heard and was experiencing due to that meeting.

Going home wasn't an option, for the wife and children were probably all asleep but the Holy Spirit inside of me was so strong I just had to tell someone.

This was my 'born again' experience as I now know and I went around to Philip and Anne, neighbour's of mine, and excitedly asked if I could come in and tell them of my amazing evening. I just couldn't contain myself; I just had to say and celebrate this wonderful dramatic experience.

These lovely people were always up late so they didn't mind me intruding on them. They could see I was 'on fire' in my speech, excitedly telling them of the preaching, the move of the Holy Spirit inside of me.

They knew all about the 'nutty bloke Steve Avery', whom I had previously mentioned to them, but I said to them "what he said is true, he isn't a nut at all, - it's all true"!

Philip offered a whisky to me to calm me down, they couldn't work out how or why I was so excited, and we spoke for about an hour. Amazed at what I was telling them, they could feel the enthusiasm and energy I had. I went home eventually; my life had changed that night and I was determined to go back to Steve's church and enjoy more of what had begun in me by the empowering of the Holy Spirit.

Freemasonry and the termination.

I had read two books about the ills of Freemasonry, sought the Bible to confirm the masonic errors in the ceremonies and I'd analyzed what the masonic stories depicted against what was biblical. I also had been told by Steve about the masonic father he'd had, who hadn't been very Godly at all. Yet despite all these negative facts, I still hadn't grasped the underlying reason that I shouldn't be partaking in such an institution.

My 'born again' experience enlightened me to leave in my heart, but my head thoughts were that having paid for the 5 masonic meetings of which there were still two to go, that I shouldn't waste my money. So, I did something that I'd never done before, I prayed to Jesus asking for a sign whether or not I should leave.

Not realizing it, there were two instances that were signs so clear, that soon I had absolutely no compulsion to stay at the lodge.

The first was in their second-degree ceremony, for normally I remembered all the words off by heart because I needed to perform admirably. On the very next lodge meeting I was fluffing my words, forgetting what to say and somehow got through the ceremony without too many grunts from the all-seeing masons sitting in the wings.

In the festive board (Three course dinner, plus wine and bonhomie) I usually was asked and gave a speech welcoming our visiting masons. On this night I thought I did my usually very welcoming speech, but at the end was met face to face with one of our high-ranking established masons.

He was fuming, eyes bulging at me, accusing me of giving veiled messages to the brethren.

This outburst was shocking, but I was delighted, for it confirmed my request – show me a sign – and there it was - I wrote a letter that evening resigning my membership.

Steve had said that freemasonry was demonic, and now I can say it is. It portrays a mason can get salvation through his good works, that he is the cornerstone and headstone of the building.

This way of salvation is wrong, for only through Jesus can a man be saved and that Jesus is the cornerstone and headstone of the building, it's declared in the bible. Such contradiction isn't to be treated lightly for I now know that one's destiny depends entirely upon Jesus.

I had another confirmation when I went to give one of the masons some money (a recommendation fee) for giving me a double-glazing lead which I had sold. He was someone that I was really very friendly with, his wife was also very nice and I got on with them both very well particularly in the masonic social evenings.

He asked me why I'd decided to leave and when I mentioned Jesus and the Holy Spirit experience, they both went mad. It was like I'd tipped two dead rats on their living room carpet; they were angry and humiliated, argumentative and the atmosphere became very awkward.

He flew into a rage, something I didn't expect, and she ranted something about how many relatives they'd had in their family all who were or had been good freemasons. I now know what was behind this outburst, but at the time was confused by their behaviour.

I left as amicably as I could, never to encounter them again.

I then did as Steve recommended, to destroy all occult, masonic paraphernalia and as I wasn't going to return to the masons or encourage anyone to join, so I did just that. I burned all books and paperwork that was combustible on a bonfire in the garden, the apron and any costume material that I had was cut up and put in the waste bin. In my head I thought 'what am I doing, these all-cost good money,' but in my heart I knew it was the right thing to do.

More of the Holy Spirit.

I tried to explain to my wife about what had gone on, she didn't understand and she couldn't or wouldn't comment. Deep down she thought I was having a mid-life crisis or something and would get over it. I was thirty-seven years old and certainly not having a personal crisis, breakdown or anything else.

Steve suggested that I met up with a wonderful lady, who always smiled, had a jolly chuckle in her conversation, was very welcoming and was gifted in deliverance. I phoned her up, asked to see her, went along to her house in Odiham. I said I hadn't come for any deliverance, but just wanted to see this lovely lady (who was in her 80's) and what she had to say about the 'Christian faith'.

Her name was Phyllis Hedges and we had a cup of tea and biscuits, she explained that some people need to have things 'cast off', that the demonic can affect people. She asked me if I needed prayer for casting off any spirit of freemasonry to which I said no, for as far I was concerned all things had changed in that direction. She then asked would I like prayer for anything at all whilst I was there.

I replied that I had this incredible experience at the Harlington Centre with Jonathan and Steve, but wanted to know "beyond all doubt" - even though I believed it was the Holy Spirit that had touched me so powerfully. She felt led to pray for me, and at the end I said Amen and left very cheerfully and relaxed, pleased to have shared time with her.

On that sunny day I returned to Brackenwood Windows driving down the M3, and suddenly I had tears flowing down my cheeks, tears that I couldn't stop.

I wasn't upset, it wasn't tears of joy – but a massive emotional release for which I had no explanation. I managed to keep driving and ten minutes later had arrived having composed myself. "What was that"? I thought. I now know that was inner healing done by again – the 'Holy Spirit'.

The following morning, I got up and as usual not very awake but functional, wandering around in my dressing gown. We don't have open fires; we don't smoke and are very safety conscious and don't take risks particularly with gas and inflammables. We are double glazed, don't have draughts and the house is modern and well insulated.

This particular morning, I wandered down my stairs and as I did so I heard a whoosh go past me, not loud but distinct which was confusing, but I ignored it. By the time I got to the bottom of the stairs I saw what looked like 'dry ice' smoke you get in night clubs or pop concerts hovering around me.

More confused I entered my kitchen whereupon there was more and more of this 'smoke', a smoke with no smell, light grey in colour throughout. My mind went into overdrive, what was it, where was it coming from, what could be on fire?
As the minutes passed there was more of this stuff surrounding me and engulfed in a column of pure light grey mist, I shouted to my wife who was in the kitchen reading a newspaper "What's happening"!

She calmly (I was calm but confused too) said "Your back is on fire"!

Immediately I threw off my dressing gown and thrust it to the floor, and instantaneously the smoke disappeared and there were no burn marks on my gown to suggest any fire had taken place.

Confused yet calm, I asked her what she saw and she said that she saw what looked like 'little tongues of fire' in an ark across my back. I exclaimed why weren't there any burn marks then, to which she replied "I don't know, but that's exactly what I saw". Being scientific I then lit our gas ring hob and put the dressing gown close to the flames. Immediately the fibres went black and a smell of burning occurred to which I said to my wife "well why has this happened and yet before – no burning and no smell"? She and I were confused, for we had no answer to explain what had happened.

That day I took the morning off, phoned Phyllis and told her about these outcomes to which she was just as amazed as we were. I also got the Bible out and a book called a concordance to help with quick referencing. It was there that I thought wow, my prayers with Phyllis had been answered.

Exodus 3

And the angel of the LORD appeared unto him in a flame of fire out of the midst of a bush: and he looked, and, behold, the bush burned with fire, and the **bush *was* not consumed**.

And Moses said, I will now turn aside, and see this great sight, why **the bush is not burnt**.

Joel 2 1- verse 28

And it shall come to pass afterward, *that* **I will pour out my spirit upon all flesh**; and your sons and your daughters shall prophesy, your old men shall dream dreams, your young men shall see visions:

And also upon the servants and upon the handmaids in those days will **I pour out my spirit**.

And I will shew wonders in the heavens and in the earth, blood, and **fire, and pillars of smoke**.

Acts 2:1-25

And when the day of Pentecost was fully come, they were all with one accord in one place. And suddenly there came a sound from heaven as of a rushing mighty wind, and it filled all the house where they were sitting. And there appeared unto them **cloven tongues like as of fire**, and it sat upon each of them.

Steve had introduced me to true Christianity which comes in word and power to heal, restore and ultimately deliver us to eternal life with Jesus. Jesus paid the price, it's an open invitation for us all and Steve ignited what was in himself to spread what God had placed in him.

It was for me and over the past twenty-eight years since these occurrences, that I've witnessed healings, deliverances and even preached myself, led others to the Lord Jesus and worked alongside churches and assisting evangelistic outreaches.

The mason who invited me into the lodge later left freemasonry and became a Christian and now does pastoral work.

Another mason, whom we invited to a Christian meeting, had a triple miracle. He was deaf in one ear, high blood pressure and had diabetes. All were healed and as he said 'unexpected' and his colleagues were utterly dumbfounded by what had happened.

After a long episode with my brother, you'll be pleased to know he was eventually found. After three visits to the psychiatric hospital his future looked bleak, but his recovery took off after Christians at a home group prayed in tongues over him. He now leads a normal life and you'd never know what a horrible past he'd had. Steve and Karen's prayers had been answered, sometimes it takes time, but God is faithful.

Steve opened a life so exciting and wonderful for me and I often wonder what a degenerate mess my life might have been had we not met.

Praise the Lord, thank you Steve – thank you to Jesus.

Scriptures

The following passages from the Bible were quoted in Steve's story…

James 3: 3-12

When we put bits into the mouths of horses to make them obey us, we can turn the whole animal. Or take ships as an example. Although they are so large and are driven by strong winds, they are steered by a very small rudder wherever the pilot wants to go. Likewise, the tongue is a small part of the body, but it makes great boasts. Consider what a great forest is set on fire by a small spark. The tongue also is a fire, a world of evil among the parts of the body. It corrupts the whole body, sets the whole course of one's life on fire, and is itself set on fire by hell. All kinds of animals, birds, reptiles and sea creatures are being tamed and have been tamed by mankind, but no human being can tame the tongue. It is a restless evil, full of deadly poison. With the tongue we praise our Lord and Father, and with it we curse human beings, who have been made in God's likeness. Out of the same mouth come praise and cursing. My brothers and sisters, this should not be. Can both fresh water and salt water flow from the same spring? My brothers and sisters, can a fig tree bear olives, or a grapevine bear figs? Neither can a salt spring produce fresh water.

Exodus 20: 1-17 (The 'Ten Commandments')

And God spoke all these words:

"I am the Lord your God, who brought you out of Egypt, out of the land of slavery.

“You shall have no other gods before me.

“You shall not make for yourself an image in the form of anything in heaven above or on the earth beneath or in the waters below. You shall not bow down to them or worship them; for I, the Lord your God, am a jealous God, punishing the children for the sin of the parents to the third and fourth generation of those who hate me, but showing love to a thousand generations of those who love me and keep my commandments.

“You shall not misuse the name of the Lord your God, for the Lord will not hold anyone guiltless who misuses his name.

“Remember the Sabbath day by keeping it holy. Six days you shall labour and do all your work, but the seventh day is a Sabbath to the Lord your God. On it you shall not do any work, neither you, nor your son or daughter, nor your male or female servant, nor your animals, nor any foreigner residing in your towns. For in six days the Lord made the heavens and the earth, the sea, and all that is in them, but he rested on the seventh day. Therefore the Lord blessed the Sabbath day and made it holy.

“Honour your father and your mother, so that you may live long in the land the Lord your God is giving you.

“You shall not murder.

“You shall not commit adultery.

“You shall not steal.

“You shall not give false testimony against your neighbour.

“You shall not covet your neighbour’s house. You shall not covet your neighbour’s wife, or his male or female servant, his ox or donkey, or anything that belongs to your neighbour.”

Matthew 11: 30

"For my yoke is easy and my burden is light."

John 10: 27

"My sheep listen to my voice; I know them, and they follow me."

Matthew 10: 5-8

These twelve Jesus sent out with the following instructions: "Do not go among the Gentiles or enter any town of the Samaritans. Go rather to the lost sheep of Israel. As you go, proclaim this message: 'The kingdom of heaven has come near.' Heal the sick, raise the dead, cleanse those who have leprosy, drive out demons. Freely you have received; freely give."

John 8: 31-32

To the Jews who had believed him, Jesus said, "If you hold to my teaching, you are really my disciples. Then you will know the truth, and the truth will set you free."

Revelation 20:6

Blessed and holy are those who share in the first resurrection. The second death has no power over them, but they will be priests of God and of Christ and will reign with him for a thousand years.

John 17: 15-19

"My prayer is not that you take them out of the world but that you protect them from the evil one. They are not of the world, even as I am not of it. Sanctify them by the truth; your word is truth. As you sent me into the world, I have sent them into the world. For them I sanctify myself, that they too may be truly sanctified."

Matthew 25: 14-30 (The 'Parable of the Talents')

"Again, it will be like a man going on a journey, who called his servants and entrusted his wealth to them. To one he gave five bags of gold, to another two bags, and to another one bag, each according to his ability. Then he went on his journey. The man who had received five bags of gold went at once and put his money to work and gained five bags more. So also, the one with two bags of gold gained two more. But the man who had received one bag went off, dug a hole in the ground and hid his master's money.

"After a long time the master of those servants returned and settled accounts with them. The man who had received five bags of gold brought the other five. 'Master,' he said, 'you entrusted me with five bags of gold. See, I have gained five more.'

"His master replied, 'Well done, good and faithful servant! You have been faithful with a few things; I will put you in charge of many things. Come and share your master's happiness!'"

"The man with two bags of gold also came. 'Master,' he said, 'you entrusted me with two bags of gold; see, I have gained two more.'

"His master replied, 'Well done, good and faithful servant! You have been faithful with a few things; I will put you in charge of many things. Come and share your master's happiness!'

"Then the man who had received one bag of gold came. 'Master,' he said, 'I knew that you are a hard man, harvesting where you have not sown and gathering where you have not scattered seed. So I was afraid and went out and hid your gold in the ground. See, here is what belongs to you.'

"His master replied, 'You wicked, lazy servant! So you knew that I harvest where I have not sown and gather where I have not scattered seed? Well then, you should have put my money on deposit with the bankers, so that when I returned I would have received it back with interest.

"'So take the bag of gold from him and give it to the one who has ten bags. For whoever has will be given more, and they will have an abundance. Whoever does not have, even what they have will be taken from them. And throw that worthless servant outside, into the darkness, where there will be weeping and gnashing of teeth.'"

Matthew 6: 9-15

"This, then, is how you should pray:

"'Our Father in heaven, hallowed be your name, your kingdom come, your will be done, on earth as it is in heaven. Give us today our daily bread. And forgive us our debts, as we also have forgiven our debtors. And lead us not into temptation, but deliver us from the evil one.' For if you forgive other people when they sin against you, your heavenly Father will also forgive you. But if you do not forgive others their sins, your Father will not forgive your sins."

Luke 21: 25-28

"There will be signs in the sun, moon and stars. On the earth, nations will be in anguish and perplexity at the roaring and tossing of the sea. People will faint from terror, apprehensive of what is coming on the world, for the heavenly bodies will be shaken. At that time they will see the Son of Man coming in a cloud with power and great glory. When these things begin to take place, stand up and lift up your heads, because your redemption is drawing near."

Prayer for those who have had abortions

Father,

I acknowledge that you alone have the right to give and take life. Life is from that moment of conception.

In my error I have taken a life in abortion, not recognising how serious this was.

I therefore truly repent before you of this action. I thank you Lord Jesus that when you died on the cross you paid for all my sins, including abortion, You took the penalty in my place, so that I can be forgiven.

Please forgive me now of this serious error, and wash me clean. I receive your forgiveness Lord.

In the name of Jesus I ask you to cleanse me and heal me from the spiritual and emotional consequences. I renounce Satan and all his works, and command any hold he has had on me through this to leave.

I thank you that my child is now in heaven with you.

Thank you Lord for your wonderful mercy and forgiveness.

Amen.